Read all the Colour CRACKERS books!

1 84121 244 X

1 84121 242 3

1 84121 232 6

1 84121 252 0

1 84121 258 X

1 84121 250 4

1 84121 228 8

1 84121 240 7

1 84121 238 5

1 84121 248 2

1 84121 256 3

1 84121 236 9

1 84121 246 6

1 84121 230 X

1 84121 234 2

1 84121 254 7

Tiny Tim

The Longest-Jumping Frog in the World!

Rose Impey
Shoo Rayner

ORCHARD BOOKS

ORCHARD BOOKS
96 Leonard Street, London EC2A 4XD
Orchard Books Australia
Unit 31/56 O'Riordan Street, Alexandria, NSW 2015
First published in Great Britain in 1993
This edition published in hardback in 2002
This edition published in paperback in 2003
Text © Rose Impey 1993
Illustrations © Shoo Rayner 2002
The rights of Rose Impey to be identified as the author
and Shoo Rayner as the illustrator of this work
have been asserted by them in accordance with the
Copyright, Designs and Patents Act, 1988.
A CIP catalogue record for this book is
available from the British Library.
ISBN 1 84121 862 6 (hardback)
ISBN 1 84121 240 7 (paperback)
1 3 5 7 9 10 8 6 4 2 (hardback)
1 3 5 7 9 10 8 6 4 2 (paperback)
Printed in Hong Kong.

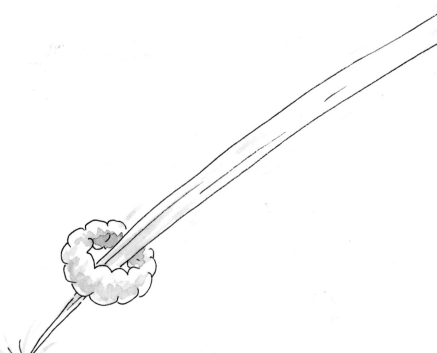

Tiny Tim

Frogs can jump.
Everybody knows that.
But how far, that's the question?

It was the middle of May.
The whole town was getting ready
for the Jumping Jubilee.
Everywhere frogs were training
for the big jump.

There were frogs leaping over lakes,

hurtling over houses,

shooting out of shops

and catapulting over car parks.

Everywhere you looked
frogs were flying through the air.

"There's going to be an accident,"
said the chief of police.
But no one listened.
Even the mayor was too busy
jumping over a traffic jam.

The champion jumper
was Rosie the Ribeter.
She had won the Jumping Jubilee
five times.

She could jump six and a half metres.
It was a record.

Even Fanny, the Flying Phenomenon,
couldn't beat Rosie.

Rosie was big, for a frog.
She was from a big family.
She had three big brothers
and a big sister.
And a big mum and dad.
They all helped to run
the Jumping Jubilee.

Her big brother Robbie
took the money.

Her big brother Ricky
announced the jumps.

Her big brother Raymond
measured the jumps.

And her big sister Roseanne
made the tea.

Rosie's mum and dad just watched.
Mostly, they liked to watch
Rosie win.
No matter how hard
the other frogs tried
Rosie *always* won.
She was the best –
up to now.

But there was one frog
who thought he could beat her.
His name was Tiny Tim.
He was really tiny.
But you should have seen him jump!

Tiny Tim had been jumping
since he was born.
As soon as he was out of his cot,
he jumped over it.

He jumped over his desk at school.
He nearly jumped over the school.

And he didn't only do high jumps.
He could do long jumps too.

Tiny Tim had set his heart
on winning the Jumping Jubilee.

But each time he tried
they wouldn't let him in.
"How old are you?" said Robbie.
"Five," said Tiny Tim.
"Five! Is that all?" said Robbie.
"You have to be six to jump.
That is the rule.

And rules are rules.
Now, hop it, baby face."

Robbie was a *big* frog
so Tiny Tim hopped it.

The next year Tiny Tim tried again.
"I'm six now," he said,
"and I want to jump."
"No chance," said Robbie.

"No spotty frogs allowed.
That is the rule.
And rules are rules.
Clear off, spotty."

Robbie was a *big* frog
so Tiny Tim cleared off.

Next year Tiny Tim tried again.
This time he was striped –
red and green.
"Haven't I seen you before?"
said Robbie.
"I'm seven and I'm striped,"
said Tiny Tim, "and I want to jump."
"You're a boy," said Robbie.

"No boys allowed.
That is the rule.
And rules are rules.
Now, get lost, laddie."

Robbie was a *big* frog
so Tiny Tim got lost.

The next time Tiny Tim tried,
all his family came with him –
and all his friends.
"My name is Tammy," he lied.
"I'm eight years old,
I'm a striped frog
and I want to jump. Now!"

"That's right," said all his family
and all his friends.
"Tammy wants to jump!"

NOW!

"OK! OK!" said Robbie.
"No problem. Come right in.
Everybody welcome."
Robbie was a big frog
but he wasn't *that* big.

At last, Ricky announced
the main jump.

Tiny Tim took his place.

"First long jumper –
Rosie the Ribeter," said Ricky.
"On your marks. Get set. Go!"

"Ribet. Ribet. Ribet," said Rosie.
Rosie jumped one – two – three.

Hooray!

She jumped six metres fifty-five!
It was a good jump.
It was a new record.
The crowd cheered.

Next came Fanny, the Flying
Phenomenon.

Well done!

She jumped one – two – three.
She jumped six metres exactly.
It was a good jump,
but not good enough.
The crowd cheered,
but not as loud.

Good try!

Then Tiny Tim jumped.
The crowd couldn't believe their eyes.
He almost flew through the air.
He jumped one – two – three.

Raymond measured it.
Tiny Tim jumped ten metres three!

Raymond measured it again,
and again. But he couldn't
make it shorter. Tiny Tim had won.
The crowd cheered and stamped
their feet.

Rosie didn't cheer.
Nor did Rosie's family.
"You can't win," said Rosie.
"Why not?" said Tiny Tim.
"You're too small."

"*Too small?*" said Tiny Tim.
"How tall are you?" said Rosie.
"Seven and a half centimetres,"
said Tiny Tim.
"All jumping frogs must be
ten centimetres tall," said Rosie.
"That is the rule," said Robbie.
"And rules are rules."

Robbie and Ricky and Raymond
and Roseanne and their
mum and dad cheered.
"Rosie's the winner,"
Ricky announced.

"That's not fair," said Tiny Tim.
"That's the rule," said Ricky.
"Hop it, shorty."
Ricky was a *very big* frog.
He was the biggest in the family.

But now Tiny Tim was mad.
He was so mad he started to puff up.
He puffed up his chest.

He puffed up his stomach.

He puffed up his cheeks.

He stood on his tiptoes.

Tiny Tim grew and grew and grew.
He looked as if he might burst.
"Now…measure me," he said.
"Go on, measure him," said all his
family and all his friends.
Raymond measured him.

"Ten centimetres – and a half,"
said Raymond.

"All right, you win," said Rosie.
"I know when I'm beaten."

Tiny Tim stopped growing.
"Tiny Tim is the winner," said Ricky.
"He is the champion."
The crowd cheered and stamped
their feet.

"Next year," said Tiny Tim,
"because I am the champion
I will make the rules.
And the only rule will be
'*no more rules*'!"

Crack-A-Joke

What goes *dot-dot-dot, croak?*
A morse toad!

What do frogs like to eat?
Lolly hops!

What's brown on the outside, green on the inside, and hops?
A frog sandwich!

What do frogs like to drink?
Croak-a-Cola!

TOAD-IN-THE-HOLE

Where does a frog hang up his hat and coat?

In the croakroom.

There are 16 Colour Crackers books.
Collect them all!

❏ A Birthday for Bluebell	1 84121 228 8	£3.99
❏ A Fortune for Yo-Yo	1 84121 230 X	£3.99
❏ A Medal for Poppy	1 84121 244 X	£3.99
❏ Hot Dog Harris	1 84121 232 6	£3.99
❏ Long Live Roberto	1 84121 246 6	£3.99
❏ Open Wide, Wilbur	1 84121 248 2	£3.99
❏ Phew, Sidney!	1 84121 234 2	£3.99
❏ Pipe Down, Prudle!	1 84121 250 4	£3.99
❏ Precious Potter	1 84121 236 9	£3.99
❏ Rhode Island Roy	1 84121 252 0	£3.99
❏ Sleepy Sammy	1 84121 238 5	£3.99
❏ Stella's Staying Put	1 84121 254 7	£3.99
❏ Tiny Tim	1 84121 240 7	£3.99
❏ Too Many Babies	1 84121 242 3	£3.99
❏ We Want William!	1 84121 256 3	£3.99
❏ Welcome Home, Barney	1 84121 258 X	£3.99

Colour Crackers are available from all good bookshops,
or can be ordered direct from the publisher:
Orchard Books, PO BOX 29, Douglas IM99 1BQ
Credit card orders please telephone 01624 836000 or fax 01624 837033
or e-mail: bookshop@enterprise.net for details.
To order please quote title, author and ISBN and your full name and address.
Cheques and postal orders should be made payable to 'Bookpost plc'.
Postage and packing is FREE within the UK
(overseas customers should add £1.00 per book).
Prices and availability are subject to change.

1 84121 244 X

1 84121 240 7

1 84121 238 5

1 84121 252 0

1 84121 256 3

1 84121 236 9

1 84121 228 8

1 84121 230 X

1 84121 234 2

1 84121 248 2

1 84121 242 3

1 84121 232 6

1 84121 246 6

1 84121 258 X

1 84121 250 4

1 84121 254 7

Read all the Colour CRACKERS books!

Collect all the
Colour Crackers!